Salt and Pepper
Jump, Jump, Jump

Mama Salt-Pepper
Photos: Jean-Marie French

Thank you to everyone who loves us!

First came Salt.

 # Then came Pepper.

And now,

they are ALWAYS together!

Salt and Pepper love to jump!

They jump high and they jump low.

They jump fast and they jump slow!

Stop, Salt!
Stop, Pepper!

Salt and Pepper, want to leap.
They want to leap like little sheep!

They leap with a whisper and then with a shout!

Stop, Salt!
Stop, Pepper!

no!

no!

no!

Salt and Pepper, just want to bounce! They hop like bunnies all around the house!

So, they bounce.

They bounce at night and during the day.

They bounce at work and then at play!

Stop, Salt!
Stop, Pepper!

First they jump high and they jump low. They jump fast and they jump slow!

Next they leap in and they leap out. They leap with a whisper and then with a shout!

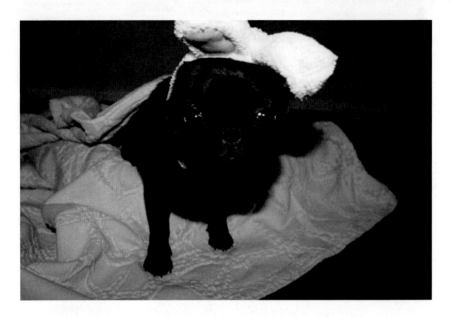

Then they bounce at night and during the day. They bounce at work and then at play! 🐰🐰

Last, they soar! Jumping

more and more and more!

**Stop, Salt!
Stop, Pepper!
It's time for a
rest!**

Yes, yes, yes!
Mama does know best.
Salt and Pepper jump into
mama's lap.

First for a hug and then
for a nap.

Salt and Pepper are ALWAYS together.

What will they do next?

Made in the USA
Columbia, SC
01 December 2022

72430376R00015